Readers often ask us if Tashi is real. We say that he's very real to us! But one thing is definitely true: the history behind this story.

You see, it was like this. One day, Barbara was reading an amazing book about the Eighth Wonder of the World – that is, the ancient clay warriors and horses of the Qin Dynasty in China. She discovered that about 8000 of these life-size terracotta figures were dug up in north-west China. The terracotta sculptures look so real that just the pictures of them are enough to make your spine tingle. Have a look at the figure on the front cover. Don't you feel that if you just touched him, he might blink?

The ancient warriors were found next to the tomb of the first Chinese Emperor, Shi, who lived about 2000 years ago. When Barbara saw pictures of these, she decided yes, this had to be a Tashi story. We saw our Tashi discovering an ancient tomb on a night without stars, and a baron creeping up behind him, a wicked baron who would do anything, anything to get his hands on that treasure...

ANNA AND BARBARA FIENBERG

When Anna and Barbara Fienberg plan a new adventure for Tashi, they have to dream up tall stories and creative fibs. Because Tashi tells fantastic stories, and everyone wants to hear his latest tale.

Anna Fienberg is a storyteller with a gift for magic and fantasy. Kim Gamble is one of Australia's favourite illustrators for children. For ten years they have been working together to produce such wonderful books as *The Magnificent Nose and Other Marvels*, *The Hottest Boy Who Ever Lived*, the *Tashi* series, the *Minton* picture books, and *Joseph*.

For Len, my great encourager,
with love B.F.

First published in 2003

Allen & Unwin
83 Alexander Street
Crows Nest 2065
Australia
Phone: (61 2) 8425 0100
Fax: (61 2) 9906 2218
Email: info@allenandunwin.com
Web: www.allenandunwin.com

National Library of Australia
Cataloguing-in-Publication entry:

Fienberg, Anna.

Tashi and the royal tomb.

ISBN 1 74114 090 0.

1. Tashi (Fictitious character) – Juvenile fiction.
I. Gamble, Kim. II. Fienberg, Anna. III. Title.

A823.3

Typeset in Sabon by Tou-Can Design
Printed in Australia by McPherson's Printing Group

10 9 8 7 6 5 4 3 2

Tashi

and the
ROYAL
TOMB

written by
Anna Fienberg
and
Barbara Fienberg
•

illustrated by
Kim Gamble

ALLEN&UNWIN

When Jack and Tashi raced to the classroom one Monday morning, they screeched to a halt at the door. Was this the right room? The walls were splashed with paintings of pyramids, mummies lying in tombs, strange writing made up of little pictures. From the ceiling hung masks of jackals and fierce-looking kings, and the heavy air smelled sweet, musty like Jack's jumper drawer where Mum kept a bag of dried flowers.

1

'Look!' cried Jack, pointing to gold pots of incense burning on the windowsill. The smoke hung in a curtain above their heads, mysterious, exotic.

'In ancient Egypt,' Mrs Hall, the teacher, said grandly as she swept into the room, 'pharaohs were buried in mansions of eternity –'

'Pyramids!' called out Angus Figment.

'Magnificent tombs,' agreed Mrs Hall, 'with burial chambers inside, filled with everything the king might need for the afterlife –'

'And the pharaohs were made into mummies before they were buried,' put in Angus Figment. 'All their livers and stomachs and whatnot were pulled out first, and then the bodies were washed with palm wine and covered with salt, and the priests used to burn incense to take away the pong because all the gasses in the bodies must have stunk like crazy –'

'Thank you, Angus,' said Mrs Hall.

Angus looked around the room happily. He'd been mad on ancient Egypt since kindergarten, and knew all sorts of interesting details about burial methods and coffins. His mother had grown worried about him in Year 1 when he'd talked about embalming the cat, but the school counsellor told her Angus just had a terrific imagination, and soon he'd move on to other things. His mother (and the cat) were still waiting.

'The Viking kings used to have their slaves and warriors buried with them,' Jack put in.

'Back in my country,' Tashi said quietly, 'we had tombs, too.'

Mrs Hall looked at him. Her eyes were round with interest. 'Did you ever see any?' she asked. 'Were there any ancient burial sites near your village?'

'Oh yes,' said Tashi. 'A royal tomb was discovered, and I was nearly buried alive in it!'

'Like a Viking slave!' cried Jack. 'Tell us what happened!'

'Yes,' said Mrs Hall, eagerly pulling up her chair near Tashi. 'Please do.'

'Well,' said Tashi, 'it was like this. Big Uncle had decided he needed a new well. You see, he lived quite far from the village and his wife was tired of having to trudge all that way for their water. So he asked our family to help him dig a new well on his land. Of course, when I told the teacher that I had to miss a day at school, Ah Chu and Lotus Blossom wanted to come too and help.'

'And did they?' asked Jack enviously.

'Oh yes,' said Tashi. 'You know how Lotus Blossom always gets her way. It was fun at first. We poked about in the soil, the men carried away buckets of stones and we built castles with them – that is until Ah Chu sat on them to eat his lunch.

'But the really thrilling part came when the men dug deeper and began to scoop out marvellous treasures, one after the other.

'Ah Chu found a bowl decorated with a golden dragon and then, right next to me, Lotus Blossom gently brushed the soil away from a beautiful bronze tiger.

'When Big Uncle himself uncovered a full-sized terracotta warrior, he told everybody to stop work.

'"This looks like an important find," he said. "We'll have to send word to the museum in the city and let the archaeologists come out and see it."

'Well, I was disappointed – I'd been hoping to find some exciting thing, too. I stepped over to look more closely at the warrior's battle robe and touch the scarf around his neck. I examined the warrior's face, and looked into his eyes. And then, it was spooky, everything around me went still for a moment, like when the wind stops in the middle of a storm. I could have sworn the warrior was holding my gaze. There was a circle of silence around us, with just our eyes speaking.

'"What?" I whispered, and perhaps I heard a faint sound. But now Big Uncle and my father bustled up to move everyone away from the digging and to fence it off with a rope.

'Just then, too late, the Baron came charging up the hill. "What's this I hear?" he shouted. "I don't believe it! A burial site found here on your land?"'

'Typical,' groaned Jack. 'That selfish money-bags ruins everything!'

'Yes,' agreed Tashi. 'He's got snake oil running in his veins instead of blood, I bet. Well, he blustered "Why wasn't I told?" and "This will be worth a fortune! To think, the number of times I've crossed this very field, never suspecting what was lying under my feet."

'"Well, if it is a King's tomb," my father said gravely, "the government will claim it, you know. It won't be *our* fortune."

'The Baron looked at us with contempt. "These people simply have no idea," I heard him mutter to himself. No one was supposed to go near the dig until the experts from the city arrived, but the Baron jumped the rope fence and went in to take a good look around.

'Big Uncle gloomily went searching for another spot for his well and I *tried* to be patient. But I kept picturing the warrior's eyes and how he seemed to be speaking to me.

'On the fifth day, the team of archaeologists from the city arrived, and they were very excited. "This is a small tomb," Director Han explained, "but very important."

'Teacher Pang had brought the whole school up to hear the verdict and nearly everyone else in the village had followed. They crowded closer to listen.

13

'"We'll dig out this fallen soil and restore the walls and the brick floor of the tomb, and then we'll put all the warriors and their swords and things back just as they were," Director Han told them. "Unfortunately, as often happens, it seems the King's burial chamber itself has been robbed and destroyed, but there are still many precious things here in the outer tomb. I'm sure we will find more."

'Teacher Pang was excited. "Imagine, children, we'll be able to step into the tomb and go back two thousand years in time!"'

'How *marvellous*!' Mrs Hall couldn't help exclaiming, knocking Tashi's pencils off the desk. 'Do you know, when the Great Pyramid was opened up, hot air rushed out and an Egyptian archaeologist said, "I smelt incense... I smelt time... I smelt centuries... I smelt history itself!" *Imagine*, children, what that would be like!'

'I'm going to be an archaeologist when I grow up,' said Angus Figment.

'Well,' Tashi went on, 'several people from the village were given jobs digging, and I begged so hard that Director Han said I could be in charge of the teapot for the men's refreshments. This meant I often passed by my particular warrior, and always I felt the soldier's eyes were following me. But there was so much to see and do, with amazing finds each day: strange coins, weapons, buckles of gold, and even a terracotta chariot and horses.

16

'So it wasn't until the dig was almost finished that I felt the pull of the warrior's gaze. Glancing around to make sure no one was near, I knelt down and whispered to him, "What is it?"

'To my amazement, I heard a faint voice: "*Help me.*"

'"How? How can I help?"

'"My wife has just been unearthed over there by the chariot. I will never be able to rest until we are standing side by side."

'"That can't be," I told him, "there aren't any women in the tomb."

17

'"My wife dressed as a warrior. No one suspected she was a girl. We were part of the King's guard, and after I discovered her secret I fell in love with her and we married. Could you bring her over to my side so that we will have at least this short time together?"

'I thought for a moment. It was fine in the day when all the workers were talking and singing around me, but I must say I didn't like the idea of coming to the tomb at night. Still, I heard myself saying, "All right, I'll come back after dark when everyone has gone home."

'I was really glad there weren't any
ghosts about when I arrived at the dig
that night. I had great trouble finding the
warrior-wife, even with the lantern I'd
brought, and still more trouble lifting her
into a wheelbarrow that luckily was
lying about.

'I saw the warrior's eyes glow with joy.
I was just unloading her beside him when
I heard voices. So I ducked down behind
a rock and waited.

'The light of the lanterns lit the faces
of three men as they drew near. I gave a
little snort of disgust. Of course! Who else
would it be, to come robbing the tomb?
The beastly Baron. He and two of his men
were arguing. The men were saying that it
was unlucky and dangerous to steal from
a tomb.

'"Nonsense!" snapped the Baron. "No one has even seen these golden drinking vessels yet, so they won't even know they're missing."

'The men very reluctantly agreed to do what he wanted and they moved closer to where I was hiding. I jumped back and stumbled on a stone. Wah!

'In the blink of an eye the men seized me, and just as I'd said a moment before about *him*, the Baron growled, "Who else would it be? Why is this boy always under my feet plaguing me?"

'"What do you want us to do with him?" asked the fiercer of the two men.

'The Baron considered and looked at the sky. "It's growing light – too late to get rid of him now. Tie him up and gag him, and put him in a corner at the back of the site." He threw a piece of carpet to one of the men to cover me and told me, "Someone will be watching you every minute – one movement and it will be your last."

'Then the men bundled me up and stashed me away as if I were nothing but a bag of old rags.

'"We'll have to leave the sack of golden goblets here for now," I heard one of them say. "Put them back under the warrior's feet. Now let's go. That Han always arrives at first light, and the diggers from the village won't be far behind."

'The morning crept on. The sun rose
high in the sky, glaring down on me. My
throat was so dry it felt as if it had been
scraped with sandpaper. My tongue grew
huge in my mouth. I could hardly breathe
under the heavy dusty carpet and although
I sneezed several times, no one heard
because of the tight gag over my mouth.
The cords around my wrist cut into my
skin. And all the time, when I wasn't
dreaming of water, oh beautiful water,
I was thinking, just how were they going to
"get rid of me"?

'My brain was hurting with trying to think of a way to raise help. And how could I think properly when there was this strange voice in my head telling me to "Push back, push back . . ." What did it mean? The voice was inside me, but it wasn't my own. It was as if someone else had got hold of my head and was telling me what to think.

'I could hear Lotus Blossom and Ah Chu, sometimes passing so close, calling my name, asking if anyone had seen Tashi.

'"It's not like Tashi to just disappear, leaving us with no tea," Big Uncle grumbled.

'By late afternoon, only the last two warriors needed to be moved back into place. The Baron's men made sure they were there on the spot. "It will be dark in a moment," they pointed out to Director Han. "Perhaps it would be better to start throwing the rubbish over the cliff and leave the two warriors till morning? We don't want to drop them because we can't see what we're doing."

'"Yes, I agree," Director Han nodded, "and we'll cover the rubbish up with soil before we go."

'"*Waaah!*" I screamed silently under my carpet. "They'll dump me over the cliff with the rubbish. If I don't die from the fall, I'll be buried alive under the soil." And all the time the strange voice in my head was growing stronger – it was shouting now, "Push *back*!" I could no longer ignore it. I focussed my mind on the voice. And as I listened, a picture came into my mind. I saw the eyes of my warrior – they were wide and staring at a small ledge jutting out of the wall behind me. "*Push back*," he said to me urgently.

'I pushed back into the wall of the tomb. Something moved behind me. A door was opening in the thick stone wall. There was nothing to hang onto and I fell backwards down a flight of steps into the darkness of a small room.

'By the dim light coming from the open door above, I could see that I had fallen down into the King's secret burial chamber. I saw an open coffin, and inside lay a skeleton in a magnificent jade burial suit. My heart leapt, but there was no time to look further. I glanced around quickly. There were two crossed swords at the foot of the coffin. I rolled myself over to one, and pushed it up against the edge of the coffin with my shoulder. Then I began to saw at the cords around my wrists. The sword was as sharp as it must have been two thousand years ago.

'In a moment my arms were free.
Quickly I released my ankles and pulled
away my gag. The relief! But there was
no time to waste. I could hear footsteps
running towards me.

'The Baron's men were at the doorway.
I saw in horror that they were starting to
close the door on me – they wanted to seal
me in the tomb with the dead King! A bolt
of fear sent me hurtling up the stairs like
lightning, yelling and screaming, "Ai-eee!
Help! Down here!"

'"That's Tashi calling!" I heard Lotus Blossom shouting, "Over here, everyone!"

'They came bursting through the doorway, ducking around the Baron's men, who suddenly remembered their wives wanted them somewhere else. The Baron was close behind them but when he heard Big Uncle and Director Han hurrying down after him, he called out, "So this is where you have been, Tashi. We were looking everywhere for you."

 'I gave the Baron a long hard stare.'

'I would have given him a great hard kick!' exploded Jack.

 'I would have cut out his organs and put them in a canopic jar!' cried Angus Figment.

'What's a canopic jar?' asked Jack.

'The thing was,' Tashi went on, 'I had no real proof that the Baron had been stealing from the tomb and meant to kill me. There was nothing concrete, really, so when I finally answered him, I said, "Yes, this is where I've been," and raising my voice so that everyone could hear, "and before I found the King's tomb, I came across a big sack of golden goblets. You'll find it over there, buried by the last two warriors."

'The Baron's jaw dropped. "What a clever Tashi," he said quietly.

'But Director Han paid no attention
to them. He was skipping about the secret
tomb, crooning with delight over the richly
decorated burial chamber and the jade suit.'

'So it was you, Tashi, who made the
most important find,' crowed Jack. 'Just
think, the *King's* tomb.'

'Well,' said Tashi modestly, 'the inner
tomb did make the find complete. Director
Han was given a promotion and he
presented our family with jobs and free
passes to the tomb for the rest of our lives.
My two warriors still stand side by side
and every time I visit them, their eyes
seem to glow with happiness.'

There was silence in the classroom for a moment as everyone tried to imagine the tomb, and the treasures, and warrior love beyond the grave.

'Did they used to mummify kings in your country, Tashi?' asked Angus Figment.

'No,' replied Tashi. 'They buried them in these splendid tombs.'

'Oh,' said Angus thoughtfully. 'Because in Egypt, well, they used to mummify all sorts of things. Even cats. Of course when the cats were dug up in my great-grandfather's time, most of them were made into garden fertiliser.'

'Thank you, Angus,' said Mrs Hall, 'and now, if you can manage not to turn our stomachs any further, perhaps you would like to share with us some more of your interesting facts about the ancient people of Egypt.'

Angus did like, and his information about Egyptian medicines and the hooks used for removing brains from mummies was enjoyed by all – well, everyone except Alex Pickle, who was sick into the potplant in the corner.

THE BOOK OF SPELLS

'What are you going to do for your
project on ancient Egypt?' Dad asked Jack
one afternoon.

'I don't know yet,' said Jack, scratching
his head. 'Angus Figment is writing a Book
of the Dead.'

'Good heavens,' said Mum, coming into
the room. 'What does his mother say
about that?'

'She thinks it's fascinating, actually,'
said Jack. 'See, the Egyptians used to write
magic spells on sheets of papyrus, and put
them inside the tombs with the mummies.
That way, people's afterlife was sure to
be happy and safe.'

37

'How can you be safe when you're dead?' asked Dad.

Jack sighed. 'The Egyptians believed in the *afterlife*, Dad. It's, like, you go on existing somewhere else.'

'Hmm,' frowned Dad. 'I don't know whether the newsagency sells papyrus.'

Mum groaned. 'So what's Tashi doing, Jack?'

Jack leaned forward on his chair. 'Well, he hasn't decided yet either, but when Angus told him about his Book, Tashi went all serious and silent.'

'Oh ho,' said Dad, drawing up his chair.
'I bet Tashi knows a thing or two about
magic spells. Are you going to tell us a
story by any chance?'

'I might,' said Jack. 'You see, in Tashi's
village the most precious possession of all
was the Book of Spells. But you might say
it was a book of *life*, because it was filled
with the most marvellous cures for all
kinds of diseases and problems. The Book
had to be guarded day and night. But one
dreadful day, it disappeared.'

'Who would take it?' asked Dad.
'A bandit? A *demon*?'

'Well, it was like this. One morning
Tashi's mother gave him a pot of soup
to take up to Wise-as-an-Owl, who hadn't
been very well lately. Tashi knocked at
the door, and waited.

'"Come in, Tashi," called Wise-as-an-
Owl from behind the door. He somehow
always knew when Tashi was there.

'When Tashi stepped into the room,
he saw someone else sitting with his
old friend.

'"Ah, Tashi," Wise-as-an-Owl beamed, "see who has come from the city to visit me! My son and I have decided that it's high time he began his study of plants and medicines if he is to take up the work of the Keeper of the Book after me." The old man's eyes twinkled. "My Son with Much-to-Learn will stay with me until he finds a house where he and his family can live."

'Tashi bowed and put his pot on the table. He politely asked Much-to-Learn about his home in the city, and his children, but all the while he couldn't help looking at the Book that lay on the desk before him. It was richly bound in red leather, with ancient glowing letters on the cover. Tashi fingered the fine brass clasp and lock that could only be opened by the golden key Wise-as-an-Owl wore around his neck.

'Tashi couldn't remember a time when the Book was not part of his life. Over the years, he'd watched while his friend had consulted it for cures of illness, pestilence and heartache. Tashi knew whole passages by heart. But later, on the way home, he felt glad that, now Wise-as-an-Owl was growing frail, his son should have come to study and work with him.

'Tashi was curious to see how Much-to-Learn was getting on with his study, but the next week, when he called, a terrible sight met his eyes.

'Wise-as-an-Owl was sitting rocking backwards and forwards in his chair, tearing his thin white hair while his son tried to calm him.

'"What is it? What has happened?" cried Tashi.

'"Someone has stolen the Book," groaned Wise-as-an-Owl. "We have

searched the house a dozen times. It's just
disappeared. Yesterday we were studying
the cure for warts and wax-in-the-ear
when there was a shuffling noise outside.
We went to investigate and when we came
back, the Book – which I had left right
here on the desk – was gone!"

'He slumped down on his stool. "I have
spent a lifetime studying it, Tashi, but
there are always new cures to find in the

44

Book, new spells to help poor souls –
whatever will we do?"

'Tashi came close and put his hand
on the old man's shoulder. "I will find
the Book for you, Wise-as-an-Owl,"
he promised.

'As Tashi was walking home, he was
so deep in thought he didn't hear Lotus
Blossom and Ah Chu running up behind
him until they were almost on top of him.
He shoved them off, saying gruffly, "I can't
come and play now!"

'Lotus Blossom shoved him back so hard that Tashi stumbled. "Why so high and mighty, Lord Tashi?"

'"Leave him alone," said Ah Chu. "You can see there's something wrong with Tashi if you'd just bother to look. He probably hasn't had his lunch yet and his stomach is growling. Mine is."

'Tashi couldn't help smiling then, and he quickly told them the trouble.

'"Oh that's the worst thing I ever heard!" cried Lotus Blossom. "We'll help you."

'"Good," said Tashi. He was relieved. "We can split up and ask all through the village if anyone has seen a stranger wandering about. Meet me back at my place after lunch."

'As Lotus Blossom turned to go, she whispered, "Sorry."

'"You can't help having sharp elbows," said Tashi.

'Lotus Blossom grinned and ran off.

'Neither Tashi nor Ah Chu could find word of anyone strange about the village, but Lotus Blossom did learn something. She had been out to see Granny White Eyes, who always knew what was going on in the village. And sure enough, Granny told Lotus Blossom the bad news.

'"Tashi's Uncle Tiki Pu is back. The cobbler, Not Yet, saw him on the road passing Wise-as-an-Owl's house."

'"Oh, no!" moaned Tashi. "That Tiki Pu would sell his own grandmother for a jar of honey."

'But Lotus Blossom was looking at him steadily. "Will you be going after him, Tashi?"

'When Tashi nodded, she nudged Ah Chu. "Then we'll be coming with you. After all, the Book is precious to the whole valley."

'"Thank you," said Tashi, a bit awkwardly. "We'd better start out right away. He'll be heading back to the city I should think."

'Ah Chu cleared his throat. "Um, I'll just hurry home and get some food together. It's going to be a long afternoon and I smelt something really good being cooked this morning. Be back in ten minutes."

'Tashi couldn't carry both Lotus Blossom and Ah Chu on his magic shoes, so the three friends shared out Ah Chu's baskets and set off on foot.

'They walked quickly but it was almost dinner time before they came across Tiki Pu standing on the river bank. He was deep in conversation with one of the river pirates, and he seemed very busy winking and grinning.

'Tashi sprang forward but, to his surprise, it was the pirate who handed Tiki Pu a bulky parcel and pocketed a bag of coins in return. Whatever he was up to, Tiki Pu wasn't selling the Book of Spells.

'They waited until Tiki Pu was alone and then Tashi ran after him and told him about the missing Book.

'"Did you see anything suspicious as you passed Wise-as-an-Owl's house this morning, Uncle?"

'Tiki Pu looked thoughtful and stroked his nose. "What will you give me if I tell you?"

'"Poor Tashi," Lotus Blossom whispered loudly to Ah Chu, "having an uncle like Tiki Pu."

'Tiki Pu coughed and said loudly, "Ha ha, can't you take a joke, Tashi? Where's the fun if we can't have a joke amongst friends? Yes, well, the only person I saw on the road was...the Baron."

'"Thank you, Uncle." Tashi swung round to his friends. "Let's go. I should have guessed. If something precious is missing, who needs suspicious strangers when we have our very own Baron at home?"

'"You thought *I'd* taken it, didn't you?" Tiki Pu said as they turned to go.

'Tashi smiled guiltily as he waved goodbye, but Tiki Pu just shrugged.

'"He's probably annoyed he didn't think of stealing it himself," Lotus Blossom sniffed.

'They were lucky enough to get a lift back to the village with a passing boat, sharing Ah Chu's delicious sticky-rice cakes and lychees with the boatman.

'"It will be quite dark before we get back to the Baron's house," Lotus Blossom said presently. They thought about this for a moment.

'Tashi nodded. "Yes, and I just hope there won't be any white tigers in his cellar this time."

'Ah Chu choked on his rice cake.

'They crept cautiously through the Baron's gardens, flinching at shadows. Ah Chu held Lotus Blossom's hand – so that she wouldn't be frightened.

'They reached the Baron's window and peered in.

'There he was, sitting at his great carved table. And what do you think he had before him? The red leather Book of Spells. The brass clasp had been broken with a poker, which lay on the table beside him, and now the Baron took a deep breath and opened the Book.

'The three friends watched his face. His jaw dropped. He turned the page. A vein began to swell on his forehead. The Baron's thick finger flipped page after page and his rage mounted, until at last he flung the Book on the floor and jumped on it. Tashi slid over the windowsill and stepped into the room.

'"Good evening, Baron. You look upset."

'"The pages are all blank!" spluttered the Baron. "There isn't a single word in the whole Book."

'"No," said Tashi. "That's because you didn't open it with the golden key that Wise-as-an-Owl wears around his neck. If the Book is opened without it, the words fade right off the pages."

'The Baron gaped at Tashi and sank down heavily onto his chair.

'"How could you?" Tashi burst out angrily. "How could you steal such a precious thing that is used to help all the village?"

57

'"Why shouldn't I?" shouted the Baron. "Why should Wise-as-an-Owl have it, just because his father had it before him? He never made a penny out of it; he doesn't deserve it."

'Tashi looked at him in wonder. It was no use talking to such a man. He picked up the Book but the Baron grabbed it out of his hands.

'"If I can't use it," shouted the Baron, "nobody will. It can burn!" And he ran to the fire.

'Tashi jumped after him, grabbing his arms, trying to reach the Book, but the Baron held it above his head.

'"You'd better let me take it back quickly, Baron," said Tashi, trying to stop the quiver in his voice. "My friends have gone up to the village to tell everyone that the Book has been found."

'Lotus Blossom and Ah Chu, who'd been peeping over the windowsill, quickly ducked their heads down.

'"We don't want a lot of people hearing that you had *stolen* it," Tashi said softly.

'The Baron lowered his arms. He thought about that. "What about the clasp? It's broken."

'"I'll take it to Not Yet. He mends locks as well as shoes these days and, if you pay him well, he might break the habit of a lifetime and do it straightaway."

'In no time at all, the Baron had agreed, Not Yet had set to work, and the Book was back in Wise-as-an-Owl's trembling hands.

'Tashi and his friends watched anxiously as he slipped his key into the brass lock and turned it. The Book fell open. White, blank pages... at first. Then slowly, as they watched, faint markings appeared; a moment more and clear black letters marched boldly up and down the pages.

'The knowledge was back where it belonged.'

'Ah,' sighed Mum with satisfaction.

'What beats me though,' said Dad, pounding his knee, 'is how that crook of a Baron stays out of jail!'

Jack smiled. 'Don't worry, Dad. I'm sure there'll be justice in the *afterlife*.'

Dad snorted and went to find a pillow to punch.